STANDA

# Fancy Nancy

# Fancy Nancy

## Ruth Craft

illustrated by Nicola Smee

COLLINS

William Collins Sons & Co Ltd
London · Glasgow · Sydney · Auckland
Toronto · Johannesburg

First published 1987
© text Ruth Craft 1987
© illustrations Nicola Smee 1987

British Library Cataloguing in Publication Data
Craft, Ruth
Fancy Nancy.
I. Title   II. Smee, Nicola
813′.54 [J]        PZ7

ISBN 0-00-184242-0

Printed and bound in Great Britain
by Mackays of Chatham Ltd, Kent

# Contents

These stories are for:
*Ellie Cook, Kathryn Alley,*
*Charlotte Naish, Sarah Jefford,*
*Katy, Jessica and Dominique Elliott.*

# 1
# Plain and Fancy

Fancy Nancy used to be called plain Nancy, but one cold November day she changed all that, and this is how it happened.

Nancy was going to start school after Christmas and one afternoon, a very cold and blustery afternoon, she set off with her mother to visit the school and Mrs Sims, who would be her teacher. Nancy was well wrapped up in her anorak and scarf and hat and her old grey chewed mittens. Nancy liked to chew the tops of her mittens so they had scraps of grey wool hanging down and they were a bit holey. But she didn't want a new pair. She liked the taste of the old ones.

It was a very cold walk to the school and Nancy was uncomfortable. She tugged her mother's arm and her mother stopped.

"I've got very bad hand pains," said Nancy.

"Let's have a look," said her mother.

It was quite hard getting Nancy's mittens off. They were very tight. Nancy's fingers were all squashed together.

"Maybe I've changed my mind," said Nancy. "Maybe I will have a pair of new mittens."

"Good," said her mother. "We'll stop on the way."

In the shop, Nancy noticed an old man buying big leather gloves with huge cuffs that came right up to his elbows. Nancy's mother took the box of mittens from the assistant and knelt down with them to show Nancy so that she could choose. But Nancy was too

busy looking at the old man's gloves.

"Pretty smart, aren't they?" said the old man. "I need them for my jaunts to the country on my Triumph Bonneville."

"What's that?" asked Nancy.

"A motor bike. A pretty fancy motor bike," said the old man.

"What's fancy?" asked Nancy.

"Well – it's smart. Good to look at. Different," said the old man.

He poked around in the box of

mittens with the end of his walking stick.

"See these mittens?" he said. "Well, some are plain and some are fancy. Those ones that are the same colour all over – they're plain. But these ones, this pair here with orange stripes and green thumbs, well, they're fancy. They're very fancy."

Nancy's mother asked her which mittens she was going to choose.

"I'll have a fancy pair," said Nancy. And she chose a pair of mittens made from all the colours of the rainbow with bright blue thumbs. Nancy stuffed her old grey mittens in her anorak pocket and put on the new ones. They were warm and there was plenty of room for her fingers and thumbs.

As Nancy and her mother walked along the road to the school Nancy could see plain cats and fancy cats, fancy dogs and plain dogs, plain cars and fancy cars, plain shoes and fancy boots. She even saw a fancy telephone box. It was square and dark grey and shining and the telephone had different kinds of buttons and numbers all in different colours. She saw a fancy baby and a plain baby. She saw fancy hats and plain coats and plain houses and

fancy houses. Now she came to look at it everything seemed either plain or fancy.

When they reached the school Nancy's mother took her to meet her teacher, Mrs Sims. Nancy noticed that Mrs Sims was wearing a plain jersey and a very fancy skirt.

Nancy's mother introduced her. "This is Nancy," she said.

"Nancy anything? Or just plain Nancy?" asked Mrs Sims.

Nancy's mother laughed and looked at Nancy. "Are you just plain Nancy?" she asked.

Nancy looked at her new mittens made from all the colours of the rainbow with bright blue thumbs.

"No," she said, "I'm fancy. I'm Fancy Nancy."

## 2
# Fancy Nancy and the Sleepless Night

Fancy Nancy had a brother. His name was Thomas and he was eighteen months old. Fancy Nancy called him Smelly Baby. Fancy Nancy had noticed that the only time Smelly Baby felt and smelled clean and fresh and lovely was just after he'd had his bath before he went to bed in the evenings. The rest of the time he smelled of old food, old drinks and old nappies.

Thomas could walk quite well but he still preferred crawling and climbing. He could crawl very fast and get from one place to the next in a matter of seconds. The skin on his knees was quite rough and hard. He could climb in and out of his cot very easily.

Once, while Fancy Nancy and her father were watching a good programme about lions on the television and Fancy Nancy's mother had gone to the cinema with a friend, Smelly Baby had got out of his cot, crawled across the landing, bundled down the stairs, crawled into the kitchen, found the cornflakes, found the soap powder and mixed the two together with a little water from the cat's bowl. He left all the mess in a pile on the kitchen floor while he crawled as fast as lightning back to his cot. When the programme about lions was over, Fancy Nancy and her father went to the kitchen to make a cup of tea. When they saw the pile of soap powder and cornflakes they were very depressed.

"I thought he was asleep," said Fancy Nancy.

"So did I," said her father.

Thomas had a room of his own and

Fancy Nancy had a room of her own with bunk beds.

One cold winter's morning, Fancy Nancy was snug in her bed, fast asleep and dreaming. It was about five o'clock. CRASH! Rat-a-tat-tat! CRASH! Fancy Nancy, half asleep and half awake, felt as if a huge, hard, heavy wardrobe with sharp corners was poking and scraping her face. Then she woke up properly and groaned. It was Smelly Baby. He was standing there, right by her pillow, with his wet nappy hanging through his plastic pants, trying to push building bricks under Fancy Nancy's pillow.

"Jumping Jehoshaphat" said Fancy Nancy, "at *this* time of night!"

Smelly Baby started to climb into Fancy Nancy's bed with his building bricks, his old tin car and an old shoebox full of dusty pine cones.

"This is too much!" said Fancy Nancy. Smelly Baby snuggled down

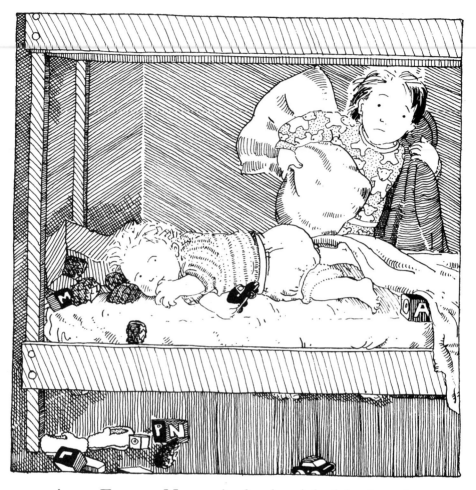

into Fancy Nancy's bed with his head
on the pine cones. Fancy Nancy took
her pillow and her blue rug and set off
to find somewhere else to sleep.

In the dark living room there was a
chippy smell. Fancy Nancy looked in
the wastepaper basket and saw crunched
up paper and two white plastic forks.

"Huh!" said Fancy Nancy, "They all had chips last night in front of the telly while I was fast asleep."

Fancy Nancy made herself a bed out of her rug and her pillow on the sofa. It was a good bed and she began to have another good sleep. Suddenly, a wet nudge bopped her on the chin. It felt as if a wet floor mop was splodging her bit by bit. First her chin, then her cheeks, then her nose, then her eyes. Fancy Nancy woke up.

"Jumping Jackeroo!" said Fancy Nancy. "The CAT!"

Puss had smelt the chip papers and had come to investigate. When she saw Fancy Nancy's bed on the sofa, she stopped to play. Fancy Nancy turned over and pushed her face into the side of the sofa. Puss climbed on her shoulder and began to nudge, nudge behind her ear.

"Is there no peace?" asked Fancy Nancy. She pushed Puss away. Puss snuggled down into the blue rug and Fancy Nancy's pillow and went to sleep.

Fancy Nancy roamed through the quiet, cold house.

Nowhere to sleep in the kitchen.

Nowhere to sleep in the breakfast room.

Nowhere to sleep in the hall.

But at the end of the hall there was the cupboard under the stairs. Fancy Nancy opened the door and turned on the light. There was the vacuum cleaner, the Christmas decorations and the ironing board. And there were all the bits and pieces the family used for camping. Sleeping bags, camp beds, the camping cooker, the big torch and a large piece of bouncy, soft foam rubber. And the old red picnic blanket.

"I've found the answer," said Fancy Nancy very quietly.

She dragged out the big piece of foam rubber and put it under the little

table in the breakfast room. She took her mother's knitting and the flowers off the little table and put them on the kitchen table. She spread the old red picnic blanket over the table so that it hung over the sides and made a tent. Then she took a sleeping bag into the tent and snuggled down in the quiet dark. Soon she was asleep.

In the morning, Fancy Nancy's mother and father were wandering about the house looking for Smelly

Baby. He wasn't in the bathroom, he wasn't in the hall and he certainly wasn't in his bed.

"Aaaaah!" they said, when they found him in Fancy Nancy's bed.

"There he is! Bless him!"

But where was Fancy Nancy?

They looked in the living room and saw her blue rug and her pillow on the sofa with Puss snuggled down and fast asleep. She was not behind the sofa and she was not behind the big chair. She was not in the bathroom or in the kitchen. But there were flowers and knitting on the kitchen table and they hadn't been there last night. The door to the cupboard under the stairs was wide open and the light was on. Fancy Nancy's father began to get upset.

"It's all right!" said Fancy Nancy's mother nervously. "She can't have gone off. She must be somewhere."

Then they saw the old red picnic blanket spread over the little table in the breakfast room.

"Ah!" they both said and pulled the blanket aside.

"Jumping Jehoshaphat!" said Fancy Nancy. "Can't a person get some sleep in this house!"

At breakfast Fancy Nancy was cross and tired. Smelly Baby threw his toast at her. Fancy Nancy cheered up when her mother and father said they must

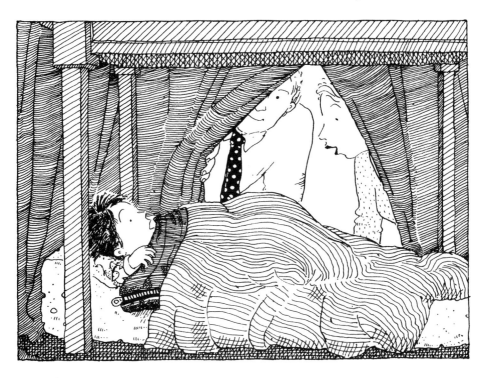

all work out a plan to stop Smelly Baby pestering Fancy Nancy in the night. They decided to put a gate across his door which he could not open and they decided to buy the gate today.

That night, after her story and her bath, Fancy Nancy went to her bedroom. On the way she stopped outside Smelly Baby's room and checked the fastening on the gate. It was nice and tight and complicated. Smelly Baby would never be able to undo that. She listened to him snoring and snuffling in his cot. She whispered to him,

"Goodnight, sleep tight
Don't let the bugs bite.
If they do, take your shoe,
Beat them till they're black and blue!"

And Fancy Nancy snuggled into her own bunk bed and went fast asleep.

# 3
# Fancy Nancy and the Long Train Journey

It was Spring and Fancy Nancy and her family were going on a long train journey to see Grandma. It was a very boring train journey. Fancy Nancy's nose was pressed right up to the window but there was nothing much to see. Only fields.

"Jumping Jehoshaphat!" said Fancy Nancy, "But *that* looks quite interesting."

She watched a farmer trying to climb over a gate. He fell off.

But the train rushed on — whizz-whizz-clacketty-clack — and Fancy Nancy couldn't see what happened next.

Fancy Nancy's mother was snoozing and her father was looking at a book with Smelly Baby.

"I'm bored!" said Fancy Nancy.

"You can go for a little walk," said her father, "Just to the end of the carriage but make sure you don't go any further. When you come back we'll have a snack."

Fancy Nancy walked down the middle of the carriage as it rushed along, whizz-whizz-clacketty-clack and she wobbled a bit from side to side. She looked at all the passengers sitting in their seats.

"That's interesting," thought Fancy Nancy, and she looked hard at two red faced men in blue suits having a row. They were waving bits of paper at each other.

"And that's quite interesting!" thought Fancy Nancy. She looked hard at two women winding knitting wool together. "And that's even more

interesting," she thought, as the woman who was holding the ball of wool dropped it. Both women dived down to pick up the ball at the same time and banged their heads together.

"And this," thought Fancy Nancy, "this looks very interesting indeed."

Fancy Nancy stared hard at an old man who was taking off his shoes carefully and rubbing his hot tired feet. The old man saw her and shook his fist at her angrily.

"Jumping Jingles!" thought Fancy Nancy. "I was only looking at your feet!"

Fancy Nancy came to the sliding door at the end of the carriage. She knew she should turn around and go back to her family, but the sliding door was half open and she longed to know what was in the next carriage. She slipped through the door and walked into the Luggage Van. It was very interesting. There were three racing bicycles with brown shiny paper wrapped around their wheels and handle bars. There was a huge heavy trunk with big locks, some square brown suitcases and a little red suitcase covered with labels. There was a box with a wooden lid and wooden rails across the front. And inside the box was a fat cat.

"Hello, cat!" said Fancy Nancy. She sat down next to the box. She could just get her fingers through the wooden rails to rub the cat's chin. She stroked and stroked and the cat smooched her hand and began to purr and purr. It was very peaceful in the Luggage Van and the cat was so warm and friendly that Fancy Nancy almost felt sleepy. Time went by.

"Jumping Jackdaws!" said Fancy

Nancy. "I'd better go back now. Good-
bye cat!"

Fancy Nancy walked through the
Luggage Van and found another
carriage, and another carriage, and
another. She could not find the old man
with tired feet, the two women winding
wool or the two angry men.

"Jumping Jellyfish!" said Fancy
Nancy to herself. "I'm lost!"

Then she remembered her father

saying the family were going to have a snack. She remembered her mother and father packing food for the journey. She remembered the rolls, the cheese and the apples. And she remembered the celery.

"Jumping Jackals!" said Fancy Nancy. "My family eat a lot of celery and they make a lot of noise while they're eating it!"

Fancy Nancy turned around and started walking the other way and she began listening for her family. She was listening for a crunchy munchy noise.

She came to a carriage and she heard a mulching squelching noise. It was the old man with the hot tired feet eating a pork pie. Then she heard a slurping noise. The two women had put their knitting away and were drinking soup out of a Thermos flask. The train rushed along, whizz-whizz-clacketty-clack.

"Be quiet, train," said Fancy Nancy.

"I can't hear my family eating celery."

She heard a glug-glugging noise and saw the two angry men drinking beer out of cans. Glug-glug-glug.

And then Fancy Nancy heard, KER-RUNCH! KER-RUNCH!

"That's my family!" said Fancy Nancy.

And sure enough, in the next lot of seats, sat Fancy Nancy's family.

Fancy Nancy's mother was chewing a big stick of celery and Fancy Nancy's father was making himself a cheese roll with a stick of celery wrapped up in the roll as well. Smelly Baby had a stick of celery but he was not eating it. He was rubbing his celery stick all over the glass of the train window and it went Squ-eeeeek!

"Hello, Fancy Nancy" said her mother. "Have some celery?" Fancy Nancy took a roll, a piece of cheese and a stick of celery.

KER-RUNCH! went Fancy Nancy

# 4
# Fancy Nancy and the Bathroom Plant

Fancy Nancy was hanging onto the pushchair when her mother crashed into a post box.

Smelly Baby bawled and all the shopping fell into the road. The cereal box broke. And the eggs broke. Fancy Nancy's mother got the cereal mixed up with the broken eggs and Fancy Nancy tried to help.

"Oh dear!" said her mother.

"It could happen to anyone!" said Fancy Nancy.

Fancy Nancy opened the new box of tissues and her mother found the new kitchen roll and they tried to clean each other up. Smelly Baby kept on bawling.

"Would the little girl like to come inside and wash her hands?" said a kind lady who was leaning over her front fence and watching them.

"I'll get cornflakes all over your taps!" said Fancy Nancy. But the lady said she didn't mind and Fancy Nancy went into her house. She went up the stairs which were very quiet and clean and into the bathroom.

The bathroom had rose-coloured wallpaper and a soft cream carpet. All the towels were folded into neat oblongs on shiny brass rails. The towels looked fluffy and soft and were exactly the same colour as the wallpaper. Soft, dry rose-coloured face cloths were folded beside them.

There was no nappy bucket.

There were no bashed up yoghurt pots or margarine tubs.

There was no big jar of baby cream standing on the side of the bath or shaving cream or toothpaste or shampoo

or plastic mugs on the shelf near the wash basin.

"Jumping Jehoshaphat!" said Fancy Nancy softly to herself. "This is remarkable!"

The lady gave her some soap and a fluffy towel. The soap was in the shape of a little orange. It was new. It smelled like an orange.

"But I'm not stupid enough to see if it tastes like an orange!" thought Fancy Nancy.

Fancy Nancy washed her hands slowly and carefully. Bits of cornflakes and egg made a gooey mess around the plug.

"Where's the cleaning stuff? Where's the pedal bin?" said Fancy Nancy. But she couldn't find the cloth and cleaner and there was no sign of a little cupboard under the basin. Fancy Nancy poked most of the gooey stuff down the plug hole with her finger and swilled out the wash basin with clean water.

Then Fancy Nancy noticed the plant.

"Jumping Jazzbands! Look at that!"

High above her head on the bathroom ceiling grew a long trailing and twining plant with green glossy leaves. It trailed and curled and the leaves were so thick that it looked as if the whole ceiling were a jungle.

"Imagine having a bath and looking up at green leaves," said Fancy Nancy to herself. "That would be remarkable."

Fancy Nancy was very quiet when her mother and Smelly Baby got home.

That night at supper, she asked her mother why their house did not have any plants.

"I've tried," said her mother.

"I just can't get them to grow," said her father.

"I mean, look at *that*!" said her mother and she pointed to a dull, small plant in a big pot on the windowsill.

"It wasn't like that when I bought it. It's got smaller and smaller and duller and duller."

"Oh," said Fancy Nancy.

The next morning Fancy Nancy was getting a carrot for her lunch from the vegetable basket when she noticed an old potato sprouting pale cream roots.

"Now that has possibilities," said

Fancy Nancy and she put the sprouting potato into a jar of water and carried it to the bathroom windowsill. Fancy Nancy watched and waited. The sprouts turned green but nothing much else happened. She watched and waited some more.

"This is not a great success," said Fancy Nancy.

The next day, Fancy Nancy was watching Mr and Mrs Higgins, the neighbours, cutting branches off their big beech tree. The leaves were thick and green and shiny.

"May I have some of those branches please, Mrs Higgins?" asked Fancy Nancy.

Fancy Nancy took the green branches into her house and lugged them upstairs to the bathroom. Her mother was washing nappies and her father was taking clean nappies off the line that hung over the bath and folding them up and putting them in the hot cupboard. Her mother and father stopped what they were doing and looked at Fancy Nancy and the branches of beech leaves.

"I suppose you want to fix your branches to the nappy line," said her mother.

"For just a few days," said her father.

"That's exactly right!" said Fancy Nancy looking very pleased.

Fancy Nancy helped her father and mother tie the green branches to the nappy line and they hauled the line up so that it swung over the bath.

That night, Smelly Baby and Fancy Nancy had their bath together. Smelly Baby played with his bashed up, old yoghurt pots and margarine tubs.

Fancy Nancy lay on her back in the warm soapy water and looked up into the green shiny leaves.

"Jumping Jehoshaphat!" said Fancy Nancy. "Now that is remarkable!"

# 5
# Fancy Nancy and the Blue Glass Bead

Fancy Nancy woke up cold in the very early morning. All her blankets were tucked up tight around her and she was wearing her warm red nightie, but her teeth chattered and her feet felt like two cold stones.

"J-j-j-jumping J-j-j-jackdaws!" whispered Fancy Nancy and she got out of bed and went to her father and mother's bedroom. They were both fast asleep in their big bed. Fancy Nancy stood shivering by her mother's pillow for a little while.

Suddenly her mother woke up and when she saw Fancy Nancy shivering and shaking, she picked her up and cuddled her. Then she put Fancy Nancy in the middle of the big bed. Fancy Nancy's father put his arms around her and her mother rubbed her cold feet with her warm hands. Fancy Nancy began to feel warm and drowsy and soon she dropped off to sleep.

When she woke up again, the big bed was empty and it was morning. She could hear her mother and father in the kitchen and she could hear Smelly Baby singing bits of Old Macdonald had a Farm and banging his spoon on the table. Fancy Nancy didn't feel cold anymore. She felt hot. Too hot! Her head felt as hot and dry as a roaring gas fire. And there was something else. Her ear throbbed and throbbed and there were cracking noises and scrunchy sounds like bits of tissue and silver paper rattling around inside her head.

Fancy Nancy's mother came in with a drink of juice and the thermometer to take Fancy Nancy's temperature. Fancy Nancy held the little bumpy end of the thermometer under her tongue and when it was time, her mother took it out and looked at the numbers by the light of the window.

"Hhhmmmn!" said her mother, "You've got a high temperature, Fancy Nancy!"

"Jumping Jalopies!" said Fancy Nancy. "And I've got a bad ear as well!"

"Hmmmmn!" said her mother and she felt around Fancy Nancy's ear while Fancy Nancy told her all about the throbbing feelings and the scrunchy sounds.

Fancy Nancy's mother told her that she was going to ring Dr Thompson and ask her to visit. While she was doing that, Smelly Baby came crawling into the bedroom with an old piece of toast. He hauled himself up to stand by the bed and put the piece of toast on

Fancy Nancy's tummy.

"Thank you, Smelly Baby!" said Fancy Nancy.

Then her father came in to say good-bye. He was off to work. He gave Fancy Nancy a hug and said he would bring her back something special from the office.

Fancy Nancy heard the doorbell ring and her mother talking. She listened

hard to see if she could work out who she was talking to. It didn't sound like Doctor Thompson. She heard a chink of glass bottles and the chink of money. It was her mother paying the milkman. A few minutes later the doorbell rang again. Fancy Nancy listened hard. She heard a nice laugh.

"That's Dr Thompson. I wonder what kind of dress she's wearing today," thought Fancy Nancy.

Dr Thompson was wearing a pretty blue dress with white daisies on the collar. She looked inside Fancy Nancy's ear with a special torch and she looked inside her throat. She listened to her chest with the stethoscope and she took her temperature. Dr Thompson told Fancy Nancy that she had a nasty infection in her ear but she'd be better soon. Then she gave Fancy Nancy a big cuddle and said she was sorry to see her so poorly.

Dr Thompson left a prescription for

Fancy Nancy and some medicine to be going on with. Fancy Nancy had two big spoonfuls straight away. The medicine tasted of mashed up bananas and yoghurt but Fancy Nancy swallowed every drop.

"Well done, Fancy Nancy!" said her mother and gave her a big drink of apple juice which tasted fresh and cool. "You can come and lie on the sofa in the living room if you like. Then I can chat to you and you can watch television if you want to," said Fancy Nancy's mother. She took some pillows off the big bed and fetched the blue rug from Fancy Nancy's bunk bed and made her a little bed on the living room sofa. Fancy Nancy settled down. The big sofa cushions were soft and bouncy. Smelly Baby crawled in to see her with his cars. He gave one car to Fancy Nancy and played quietly on the floor with the others. "Brmm! Burrum-brim," went Smelly Baby.

Fancy Nancy's mother had turned
on the television but it was not quite
time for children's programmes. Instead
there was a programme for grown ups
about lost cities. A woman was standing
in a field with a brook and a tumble-
down fence and she was explaining that
underneath the field there was probably
the remains of a lost city that had been
covered up with earth and trees and
plants and houses and gardens. Lots of
people were digging in the field with

little trowels and finding little pieces of pottery, bits of bones and animals' teeth.

"Jumping Jig-saws!" said Fancy Nancy. "I wish I was well enough to dig in our garden. I bet there's lots of interesting stuff out there. Bits of old bones. Bits of saucers and cups and plates. And beetle skeletons!"

Fancy Nancy wriggled around on the big sofa cushions.

"Jumping Jerusalem!" she said, "I

could dig up the whole back garden and find a lost city!"

Fancy Nancy poked her fingers down into the little space between the cushions and the back of the sofa. Her fingers felt something soft and whispery. She poked and pulled and prodded and pulled again and out came a sycamore seed.

"Jumping Jingles!" she said, and put the sycamore seed on her blue rug. Fancy Nancy dug some more. This time her fingers found something hard and curly. She pulled it out. It was a little sea-shell. She put it on the blue rug next to the sycamore seed.

Now Fancy Nancy put both hands down into the little space. She rummaged and poked with all her fingers and this time she found something that was cold and smooth. She pulled it out. It was a little silver whistle. So now she had a sycamore seed a shell and a little silver whistle.

"I never thought I'd find a lost city in the sofa!" said Fancy Nancy.

Fancy Nancy's head began to ache a little and she began to feel shivery again. But she thought she would have one more dig in the sofa. Her fingers scrabbled down behind the sofa cushions but they couldn't feel anything. She tried again and this time her fingers found something small and round like a hard pea. Fancy Nancy pulled it out. It was a little round blue glass bead. She put the little bead next to the sycamore seed, the shell and the little silver whistle. Then her mother came in with another drink of juice for Fancy Nancy and some more medicine.

Fancy Nancy felt a bit cross and miserable.

"Good heavens!" said Fancy Nancy's mother, looking at all the things Fancy Nancy had found in the sofa. "Where did all that come from?"

"I found them all in the sofa. But I

don't know where they were before then," said Fancy Nancy, crossly. "I feel horrible!"

Fancy Nancy's mother gave her the medicine and the drink and tucked Fancy Nancy up so that she was warm and comfortable. She took the little blue glass bead, the silver whistle, the shell and the sycamore seed and held them in one hand and stroked Fancy Nancy's head with the other.

"I remember where the sycamore seed came from," she said. "Do you remember last Autumn when we went to the Park and found all the sycamore seeds flying about in the wind? Do you remember how you brought some home and Dad showed you how to make helicopters out of them? I expect one of them flew straight towards the sofa and whizzed down behind the cushions. And that's where it stayed until you found it just now."

Fancy Nancy smiled.

"I remember," she said quietly.

"And do you remember in the summer going on the outing to the sea-side with Mrs Sims and all the things you brought home with you? Shells, stones, bits of sea-weed and a star fish? You had them all stuffed in the pockets of your jeans. You probably sat down on the sofa to watch television and one of the shells slipped out and dropped behind the cushions."

"Probably . . . probably did," whispered Fancy Nancy. "And what about the little whistle?"

"Well," said Fancy Nancy's mother, "do you remember pulling your cracker with Auntie Mollie last Christmas?"

"I remember!" said Fancy Nancy, sitting up. "I remember now! Auntie Mollie got the paper hat and I got the little whistle but I hid it down the sofa to stop Smelly Baby from swallowing it!"

"That's right!" said her mother.

Fancy Nancy took the little blue

glass bead from her mother and held it in her hand.

"What about this then?" asked Fancy Nancy and she gave a little yawn. "Where do you think this came from?"

"I don't know," said her mother.

"Is this a mystery?" said Fancy Nancy noticing how the light made the blue glass sparkle.

"That's a mystery!" said her mother.

Fancy Nancy felt warm and comfortable and sleepy. Her ear had stopped throbbing and her head stopped aching. She looked at the big arm chair in the corner of the living room. There were probably hundreds of things lost down there. "I'll have a little snooze and later on I'll have a look!" thought Fancy Nancy. She curled up in her blue blanket and with the little blue glass bead held tightly in her hand, she dropped off to sleep.

# 6
# Fancy Nancy Saves the Fish

All the people in Mrs Sims's class were busy. Some were making pictures with paint and crayons, some were making shapes with clay, some were dressing up as kings and bus-drivers and some were making dams and waterfalls at the sink with mugs, beakers and jugs. Mrs Sims was looking at some pictures and stories with the people in the book corner and Fancy Nancy, Brian and Sharon were busy in the Wendy House. They were pasting pictures on the wall to make new wallpaper and putting new curtains in the windows.

Suddenly, someone working by the sink yelled, "Help! Help!" And the people making shapes with the clay yelped, "Look! Look!" And the people dressing up as bus-drivers and kings shouted, "Mrs Sims! LOOK! LOOK!"

Fancy Nancy poked her head out of the Wendy House. She saw at once what the people were yelling, yelping and shouting about. A huge jet of water was pouring out of the bottom of the fish tank.

Fancy Nancy did not waste a minute. She undid one of the curtains from the Wendy House and tucked it under her arm. She ran fast across the room to the spouting fish tank. She soon found the little hole where the water was pouring through and she carefully poked the Wendy House curtain into the gap and held it there tight with her hands. The water stopped gushing and pouring at once.

"Quickly everybody!" said Mrs Sims. "We must save the fish. They'll die without water!" Mrs Sims filled a

big basin with clean water from the sink. She found some plastic cups and put some steady chairs by the tank. Then everyone began to take turn and turn about to rescue a fish in a paper cup, and pass it down to the next person who ran to the big basin and put the fish gently in the clean water. And all the while Fancy Nancy kept the Wendy House curtain jammed into the leaking fish tank.

"Are you tired, Fancy Nancy?" said Mrs Sims. "Shall I take over?"

"Tired?" said Fancy Nancy. "Never!"

Soon all the fish were out of the tank and swimming around the big basin. Then Mrs Sims got some buckets from the kitchen and everybody began bailing the rest of the water out of the tank and into the buckets. Fancy Nancy needed to go on holding the Wendy House curtain in place because, if she'd let go, all the water would have poured out over the classroom floor. But soon the job was done.

Mrs Sims called everybody into the book-corner for a chat and a story. Fancy Nancy's cardigan was rather wet so Mrs Sims found something else for her to wear while it was drying. It was the magic blue velvet cape from the dressing-up box. Fancy Nancy liked wearing that cape. Mrs Sims thanked everybody for helping to save the fish and she especially thanked Fancy Nancy for stopping the flood of fish tank water from pouring all over the floor of the classroom. And she told everybody about a very famous boy who lived a long time ago who had stopped the sea from flooding the fields of Holland by putting his hand in the sea-wall which had broken in a storm.

"Just like Fancy Nancy!" said everybody.

The next morning, the new fish tank arrived and was put into place. The fish had spent the night in the big basin and the children had given them a little breakfast to be going on with. Mrs Sims said they could have a proper feed when they were put into their new home. While the tank was filling up Mrs Sims called everybody together and gave them all an empty yoghurt pot. Everybody was to move one fish into the tank.

"You can have first go, Fancy Nancy," said Mrs Sims "Because you worked so hard to save the fish yesterday.

Which fish are you going to choose?"

Fancy Nancy looked at the fish. They all looked pretty much the same – neat, tidy, plain goldfish – not too big and not too small. And then she saw quite an old goldfish. His scales were a bit dark but his fins were silvery gold. He had some nice red blotches on his

back and his tail was bright golden orange. He didn't swim in a straight, plain way. He did fancy twirls and whirls slowly around the big basin.

"That's the one!" said Fancy Nancy. "That fancy fish there! He can be the first fish in the new tank!"

And Fancy Nancy caught the fancy fish gently and put him to swim in his new home. The fancy fish twirled and whirled and swirled around the tank and in and out of the waterplants. Fancy Nancy smiled.

"That's a good job well done!" said Mrs Sims and everybody brought their plain goldfish to join the old fancy goldfish swimming around the new tank.

# 7
# Fancy Nancy and the Swimming Pool

Fancy Nancy and her mother were getting ready to go for a swim on a hot summer's day. Fancy Nancy's mother was very quick at getting out of her clothes and into her swimming suit. She stuffed her clothes and her shoes into the wire basket any-old-how because she was in a hurry to get into the water. Fancy Nancy's mother liked a good swim.

Fancy Nancy liked to fold her clothes carefully, roll her socks up into little packets and stuff them into the toes of her plimsolls. Fancy Nancy and her mother took the wire baskets full of their clothes to the lady behind the counter in the changing rooms.

"Jumping Jumbles!" said Fancy Nancy. "Look at all the baskets. Look! There's someone in the pool today who wears blue trousers with white spots and someone who wears big red boots and someone who wears an old furry jacket and someone who wears a sparkly purple T-shirt . . . ."

"Come on, Fancy Nancy!" said her mother.

Fancy Nancy's mother took her to the little pool where Mrs Brown was ready to help Fancy Nancy with her swimming. Then Fancy Nancy watched her mother dive into the big pool at the deep end and begin swimming. Fancy Nancy watched her for a little while and noticed how good she was at getting out of the way of all the kickers and splashers and the very old men who swam sideways. Then she splashed into the little pool with Mrs Brown.

Mrs Brown had tight, curly black

hair and a black and orange swimsuit. She splashed in and out of the little pool helping Fancy Nancy and other people to practise their strokes, tie on their arm-bands and practise their kicking. Every so often, Mrs Brown would sing:

"Oh Jemima!
Look at your Uncle Jim.
He's in the duckpond
Learning how to swim.

First he does the breast stroke
Then he does the side,
Now he's under the water
Swimming against the tide!"

Fancy Nancy and the other people would join in the song with kicks and splashes.

Fancy Nancy began to feel a bit shivery and cold. Mrs Brown said she could get out of the water for a while,

so Fancy Nancy wrapped herself in her towel and watched her mother swimming and the people in the little pool learning to swim.

"I bet I could just get dressed all by myself," thought Fancy Nancy and off she went to the changing rooms. She collected the wire basket from the lady behind the counter, found a cubicle and pulled the heavy blue plastic curtain across the door.

It was a bit dark. And quiet.

Fancy Nancy rubbed her legs and arms hard with her towel, but when she'd dried her chest and her back, her wet hair dripped down and made her all damp again. She pulled on her knickers and her jeans. They felt dry and soft. But they felt different. She put her hands in her pockets. Her fingers found something soft and rubbery and spiky. She pulled her hand out quickly.

"I haven't got anything like that in my pocket today!" she said. Then she looked at the vest, the T-shirt and the socks and shoes in the basket.

"They're not my clothes. They're not my clothes at all," she whispered.

Fancy Nancy pulled back the heavy blue plastic curtain and peered out into the changing room. There was nobody to be seen.

Nobody else seemed to be getting dressed, or running in and out of the cubicles, or standing on the weighing machines, or drying their hair with the hair dryers. Fancy Nancy couldn't hear anything except her own breathing. She felt a big hot ache in her chest and her eyes began to prickle and sting.

And then she saw her mother.

Fancy Nancy's mother, all wet and dripping from the swimming pool, knelt down and gave Fancy Nancy a big hug.

"Somebody's changed my clothes and I've got a spiky thing in the pocket!" said Fancy Nancy.

But then Fancy Nancy's mother showed her another person who was upset. Someone else who was being hugged by her mother, someone else who'd got the wrong clothes, someone else about the same size and shape as Fancy Nancy. Someone else called Jenny.

Fancy Nancy began to feel better. She licked some of her tears off her mother's neck. They tasted good and salty.

She put her hand in the pocket of

the jeans and pulled out the soft, rubbery, spiky thing. It was a yellow rubber hedgehog.

"Jumping Jingles!" said Fancy Nancy and gave it to Jenny.

Then Jenny and Fancy Nancy swapped their baskets and their clothes. They got dressed and went off with their mothers to have a drink and a bag of crisps in the cafe.

As Fancy Nancy went past the lady behind the counter in the changing rooms she noticed that the wire basket with the sparkly purple T-shirt was still there.

"It's just as well I didn't get *that* basket!" said Fancy Nancy. "Mind you, I wouldn't mind a sparkly purple T-shirt!"

# 8
# Fancy Nancy and the Difficult Guest

Once, when Fancy Nancy and her family were on holiday, they met another family on the beach. There was a father and a mother, a girl of about the same age as Fancy Nancy and a baby a bit younger than Smelly Baby. The grown-ups used to talk a lot and laugh and swim together. Smelly Baby and the other baby took each other's toys away and gave each other sandy hugs from time to time. Fancy Nancy and the girl called Betty played next to each other on the beach by the sea.

Every day, Fancy Nancy tried to build a Town Hall out of sand, sea-weed, rocks and shells and to make a deep rushing river flow past the front door. It was a difficult piece of building to do because the tide crept up the beach during the day and the Town Hall was often completely demolished before Fancy Nancy had time to finish it.

Betty made small sandcastles and stuck small pebbles all over them.

A long time after the summer holiday was over, Betty came to stay the night at Fancy Nancy's house. She arrived after tea with an overnight bag and her father was also carrying a huge plastic carrier bag. Although it was a cold afternoon, Fancy Nancy was in the garden doing a bit of digging. She explained to Betty that she was working on a new tunnel. She showed Betty the old tunnel which had caved in and collapsed and she showed her where she'd tried to prop it up with the old plastic flower pots. It hadn't worked and there was dirt and rubble every-

where. Fancy Nancy said Betty could
make a tent, if she liked, using some old
runner bean poles and the red picnic
blanket in the cupboard under the
stairs. Betty shivered and said she'd
like to go inside and watch television.

"Jumping Jellybeans!" said Fancy
Nancy, and she went on digging.

Soon it began to get really dark and
the street lamps shone into the garden

making wonderful shadows and shifting light. Fancy Nancy went into the house to see if Betty had changed her mind. Betty was sitting in front of the television with an apple on her lap. Smelly Baby was on the floor pulling at her white socks and trying to chew them.

"Betty," said Fancy Nancy, "would you like to come outside and play in the dark?"

"No," said Betty. "And I don't want to eat this apple. And I don't like your baby."

Fancy Nancy felt a bit red and cross.

"What's in that plastic carrier bag, then?" she asked.

"Things," said Betty.

At suppertime Betty ate and ate and so did Fancy Nancy. Supper was spaghetti with meatballs and cheese and they both smacked their way through two helpings so there wasn't much time for talking.

At bathtime and at storytime they were still very quiet. When it came to bedtime, Fancy Nancy's father carried the plastic bag along to Fancy Nancy's bedroom where Betty was going to sleep in the top bunk. Betty opened up the plastic carrier bag and spread everything out all over the floor. Inside the bag was an enormous collection of stuffed toys. Some were made of velvet, some of wool, some of cotton. Some were soft, some were furry, some were shiny, some were spotty.

There were cats, dogs, sheep, monkeys, giraffes, elephants and a hippopotamus.

"They're my friends," said Betty, "And they all come into my bed."

"Jumping Jerusalem!" said Fancy Nancy, and she watched Betty climb up the little ladder to the top bunk.

Betty settled herself into the bunk pulling the bedclothes tight up to her chin.

"Now pass up the giraffes!" said Betty.

"Please. Pass up the giraffes, please," said Fancy Nancy.

And Fancy Nancy passed up the giraffes to Betty.

And then she passed up the elephants, the monkeys, the cats, the dogs and the sheep.

"What about the hippopotamus?" said Fancy Nancy.

"Henry Hippo is his name," said Betty.

"Sorry. Anyway, where does he go, because I'm getting tired of all this?" said Fancy Nancy

"He goes at the very end of the bunk. Not on my feet. At the very end of the bunk so he can rest his big back against the board," said Betty.

"Jumping Jampots!" said Fancy Nancy, and she put the hippopotamus at the very end of Betty's bunk.

Fancy Nancy's mother and father

came in to say goodnight and turn out the lights. Fancy Nancy had a special night-light in the shape of a dolphin that was never turned off.

Betty said, "That dolphin light will stop me going to sleep."

"No it won't," said Fancy Nancy, and she tried to go to sleep herself.

It was very difficult. She was not used to having someone sleeping above her and Betty seemed to toss and wriggle and that made the mattress above her whisper and creak.

Once, Fancy Nancy thought it was Betty whispering.

"What?" said Fancy Nancy.

"Nothing. I didn't say anything. Now you've woken me up," said Betty.

"Jumping Jackeroos! If you were asleep you wouldn't have heard me say 'What?'" said Fancy Nancy.

Fancy Nancy's mother put her head around the door. "Sssssshhhhhh!" she said.

"Now see what you've done!" said Betty.

"Sssssshhhhh!" whispered Fancy Nancy with her teeth clenched tightly together.

Fancy Nancy cuddled her knees up to her chin and put her arms tightly around her head. She didn't want to hear any more whispering and creaking and she couldn't stop thinking about all those stuffed animals in the bunk above her.

She drifted off to sleep, thinking about stuffed sheep.

Thump! Thump! Thump!

Fancy Nancy woke up suddenly.
Three shapes had flashed by her head.
She leaned out of her bunk to pick them
up. In the light of the dolphin lamp she
could see what they were. Three stuffed
dogs. And while she was looking at
them, five more woolly shapes crashed
around her head. Cats! Betty must
have rolled over in her sleep and
pushed the cats and dogs out.

"It's raining cats and dogs!" said
Fancy Nancy.

She got out of her bunk and went off
to look for the old red picnic blanket.

"Just as well she didn't make a tent

out of it!" thought Fancy Nancy.

She dragged it up the stairs and hauled it across her room. She reached up and tucked the long edge of the blanket all along and under Betty's mattress. Now the blanket hung down over the sides of Fancy Nancy's bunk. Now she would be safe from raining animals.

"I'm always having to make myself tents in this house!" said Fancy Nancy crossly and she went off to sleep.

In the morning, Fancy Nancy's mother came to wake Fancy Nancy and Betty. She smiled when she saw what Fancy Nancy had done with the old red blanket. She pulled it aside to say Good Morning.

"That's a pretty fancy tent you've got there!" said Fancy Nancy's mother.

"Raining cats and dogs was bad enough!" said Fancy Nancy. "But Jumping Jigsaws! What about a raining hippopotamus?"

# 9
# Fancy Nancy and the Christmas Party

Fancy Nancy was sitting on her father's lap listening to her bedtime story which was about a bee and a rabbit. It was a good story. Her father was wearing a suit which had sharp edges on the cuffs and lapels and a very white shirt which was new and had an interesting cardboard smell. Smelly Baby was fast asleep in his cot upstairs. Fancy Nancy's mother was getting dressed to go out to the Christmas Party. Suddenly the telephone rang.

Fancy Nancy's mother went to answer it. Fancy Nancy could see her in the hall. She looked very pretty in her shimmering blue dress. Fancy Nancy heard her mother say, "Oh dear. Oh dear. Well never mind." And she put the phone down and came into the sitting room looking sad and cross.

"Oh dear," said Fancy Nancy's mother, "That was Jenny the baby-sitter. She can't come to baby-sit for us tonight. She's got a bad cold and a sore throat."

"Oh," said Fancy Nancy's father.

"I like Jenny," said Fancy Nancy. "She plays wolves with me under my bunk before we put the light out."

"I wanted to go to that party," said Fancy Nancy's mother looking sad.

Fancy Nancy's father went to the telephone and closed the sitting room door. Fancy Nancy and her mother looked at each other and tried to hear what he was saying. They couldn't.

Fancy Nancy's father came back looking pleased.

"We can *all* go to the party," he said.

"What about Smelly Baby?" said Fancy Nancy. "He wouldn't be any good at a party!"

"He can sleep upstairs in their spare room," said her father.

Fancy Nancy went upstairs to her bedroom and took off her pyjamas and slippers. Her mother changed Smelly Baby's nappy and wrapped him in a big rug. Fancy Nancy put on her red spotty dress and her new sandals. Her father did up her back buttons and tidied her hair. She asked her father, "Will there be other children?"

"I'm not sure," he said.

"Oh," said Fancy Nancy.

Smelly Baby was strapped into his special seat in the back of the car and Fancy Nancy sat beside him. It was raining outside and the car was snug and warm. All the Christmas lights in the shops and the streets looked fuzzy and muzzly behind the wet windscreen. Fancy Nancy watched her father

changing the gears and her mother's
earrings bobbing up and down and
glinting in the light from the dashboard.
Smelly Baby snored and grunted.

When they came to the party there
was a lot of noise.

"Smelly Baby will wake up!" said
Fancy Nancy, but Smelly Baby slept
soundly as his mother and father took
him up to the spare room.

Fancy Nancy looked around the
Christmas party. There were no other

children. There weren't many decorations. Just one Christmas tree that was all gold with white roses on it. No sparkle. Or balloons. Or sandwiches. Or games or paper chains.

Fancy Nancy felt very small.

She was only as tall as people's handbags or trouser pockets. "I don't like this Christmas Party." said Fancy Nancy to herself.

She found a good place to sit behind a big sofa. She sat down on the soft carpet and started looking at the big books on the bookshelves. She found a good book about volcanoes, a good book about cooking and then she found an excellent book about the jungle which was like one she had at home.

There were pictures of monkeys, parrots, snakes, tigers, elephants and fever carrying insects.

Fancy Nancy got up and looked over the sofa to see how the party was getting on. She saw her mother and father chatting and they waved and smiled and said, "Are You All Right?" by moving their mouths but not saying anything out aloud. But the rest of the party seemed just the same. People talking, people laughing, people just standing about and saying nothing, people getting in each other's way and saying sorry.

"Jumping Jungles!" said Fancy Nancy. "This party is pretty boring!"

A lady with pink and orange hair squawked with laughter.

"Now that's interesting," said Fancy Nancy. She sat down on the floor and looked again at the book about the jungle.

"Squawk! Squawk!" went the lady with the pink and orange hair.

"Ha-ha-ha-ha-ha!" roared the party.

Fancy Nancy found the pictures of the parrots in the jungle.

"Jumping Jemima!" said Fancy

Nancy. "There's the squawky lady!"

And sure enough, in the book, there was a big coloured photograph of a jungle parrot with pink and orange feathers – exactly like the squawky lady's hair.

"I wonder if any of the rest of the party is in here," said Fancy Nancy, and she looked through the book and got up and looked at the party again.

A big man moved slowly through

the party. He was wearing a grey suit
and his grey tie flopped from side to
side. He had big feet and very chunky
hands.

"Elephant!" said Fancy Nancy, and
she found a picture of him in the book
about the jungle.

A tall lady in a silvery dress that
reached right down to her ankles and
right up to her ears, slowly and carefully wound her way around and

through the people. She stood behind a tall house-plant for a while and then sat lazily on a chair, tucking her feet under her.

"Snake!" said Fancy Nancy. And she found a picture of a lazy, silvery snake in the book about the jungle.

A tremendous chattering and laughing broke out in the middle of the party. Three short men in brown and fawn suits were telling each other jokes.

"Ha-ha-ha-ha-ha-ha-HAH!" they chattered.

"Monkeys!" said Fancy Nancy.

A small lady buzzed around the party offering people crisps and nuts. She had spiky grey hair and was wearing long, dangling, glittering earrings.

"I hope she's not a fever-carrying insect," said Fancy Nancy. She looked hard at the picture of the fever-carrying insect and at the lady while she took some crisps and nuts and said thank you. And then she stared at the lady's earrings. One earring was made in the shape of the sun and the other was made in the shape of the moon.

"That's fancy!" said Fancy Nancy quietly. "That's *really* fancy!"

The lady saw Fancy Nancy looking at her earrings and smiled.

"Hello," she said kindly. "Are you having a good party? I like your dress!"

"I like your *earrings*," said Fancy Nancy.

"Tell you what," said the lady. "How about wearing one. Just for the party!"

"Could I?" said Fancy Nancy. "Which one?"

"You choose," said the lady.

"I'll choose the sun please," said Fancy Nancy.

The lady unclipped the sun earring from her ear and clipped it to Fancy Nancy's. The earring was heavy and made Fancy Nancy's head feel lop-sided. The lady took a mirror out of her purse.

"Look!" she said.

Fancy Nancy looked in the little

mirror and saw the beautiful sun earring swinging from her ear and glinting and glittering in the lights.

"Jumping Jehoshaphat!" said Fancy Nancy. "Thank you. Thank you. I'll give it straight back to you when it's time for us to go home."

Fancy Nancy came out from behind the sofa and walked around the party. She smiled at the men who had looked like monkeys, the lady who looked like a snake, the man who had looked like the elephant and the lady who had looked like a squawky parrot and they smiled back. She found some interesting food laid out in the kitchen and made a big sandwich out of french bread and cold, spicy sliced ham. One of the monkey men helped her find the mustard and the squawky parrot lady made her a drink of mixed orange and apple juice with lots of ice. Every time she moved her head she felt the sun earring jingle and swing and she could see its glitter

shining back at her from the silver forks and spoons and from the big silver bowl of fruit salad. Fancy Nancy began to enjoy the party.

When it was time to go Fancy Nancy looked at her family. She looked at her mother's pretty shimmering blue dress, her father's smart suit and new white shirt and she looked at Smelly Baby, soft and pink and sleeping. She knew she would not find anybody like them in the book about the jungle.

"Time to go home," said Fancy Nancy, and she went to find the lady who had lent her the beautiful earring. Fancy Nancy covered her ear with her hand and felt all the little ridges and bumps and smooth places that the pattern of the sun made in the metal.

The lady carefully unclipped the earring and Fancy Nancy gave her a kiss.

"Merry Christmas and thank you," said Fancy Nancy.

"Merry Christmas, Fancy Nancy." said the lady.

When Fancy Nancy was at home again and tucked up in her bunk she found it hard to go to sleep. She kept thinking about the party, about the book about the jungle, about the way people looked like animals sometimes, about the cold spiced ham and the man who'd helped her find the mustard and above all about the beautiful earring. She felt she could still feel it clipped to her ear. But then she thought about that Christmas tree. That plain gold Christmas tree with nothing but white roses stuck all over it!

Tomorrow her father was going to take her to the market to buy their real green Christmas tree covered with spiky needles. Fancy Nancy began to dream of all the fancy things she would make for the tree. Gold and silver crinkly chains, red and green and silver baubles covered with glitter, lots of tinsel bows

and on the top of the tree the biggest
and fanciest silver and gold cardboard
star she could make.

And as she thought about the star
twinkling and winking in the Christmas
lights, Fancy Nancy went off to sleep.